NIGHT OUT

by Daniel Miyares

schwartz & wade books   new york

All alone.

An invitation?

THE HONOR OF YOUR PRESENCE
IS REQUESTED

A decision.

And a journey begins.

A friend.

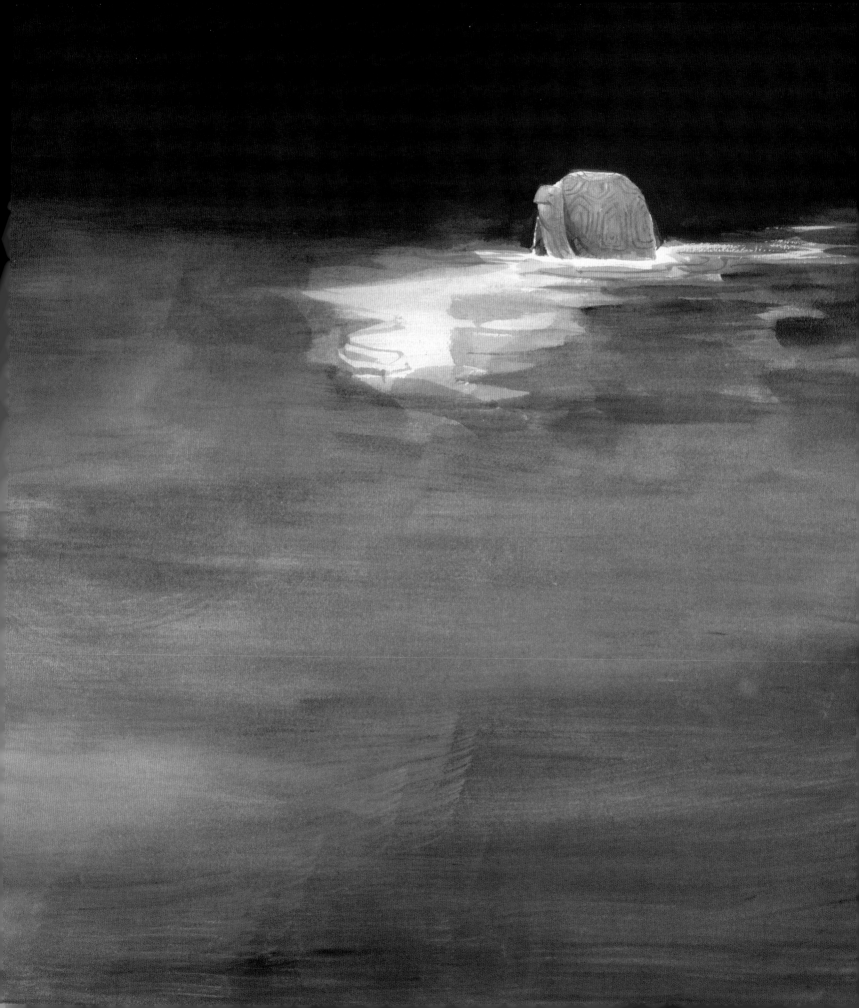

"Come in! Come in!"

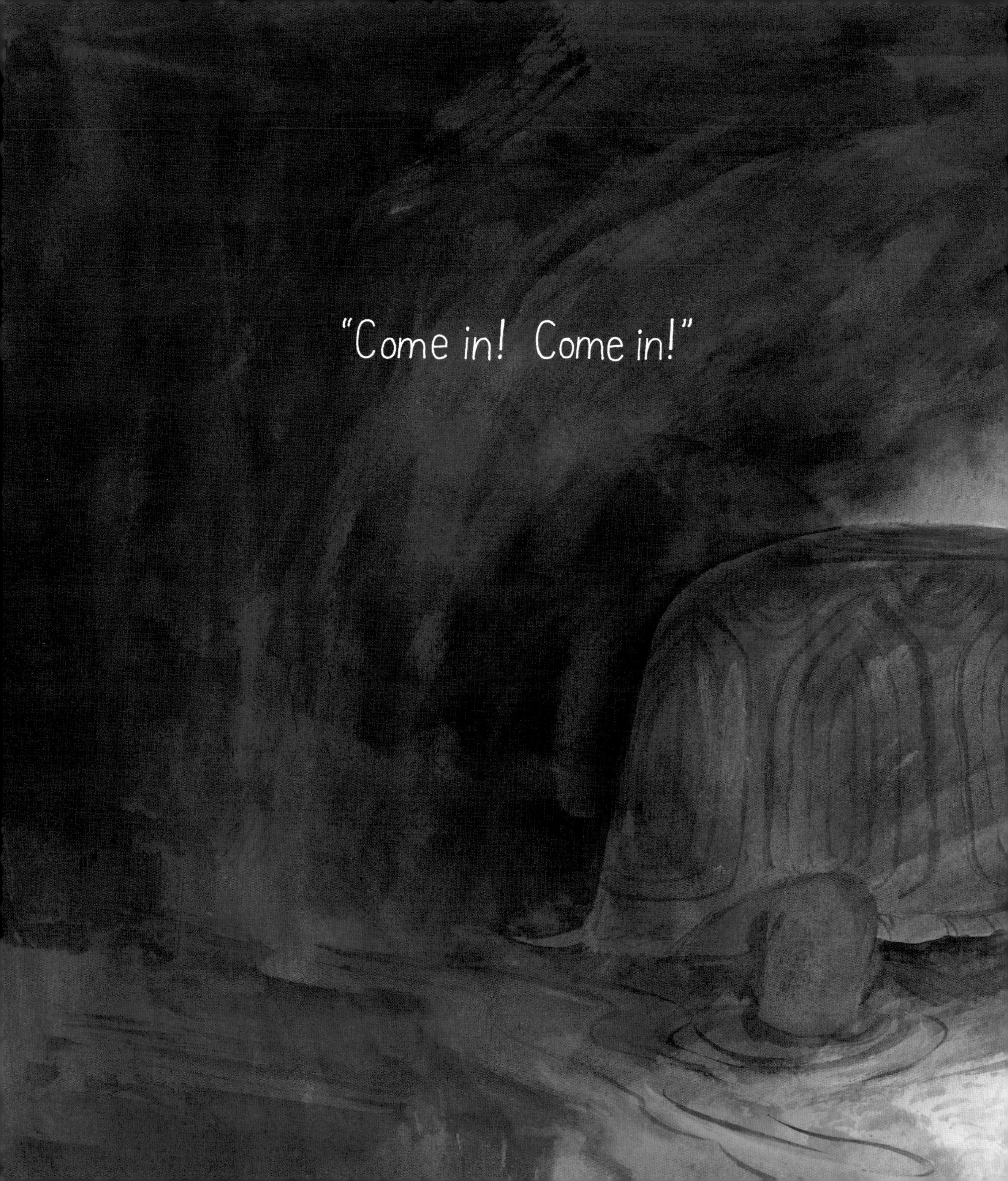

"You're just in time . . .

"And a song!"

A night out ends,

And a new day begins.

A story to share.